ANGRY ARTHUR

by Hiawyn Oram

illustrated by Satoshi Kitamura

A Sunburst Book • Farrar, Straus and Giroux

Once there was a boy named Arthur.
One night, Arthur wanted to stay up
and watch a Western on TV.

"No," said his mother.
"It's too late. Time for bed."
"I'll get angry," said Arthur.
"Get angry,"
said his mother.

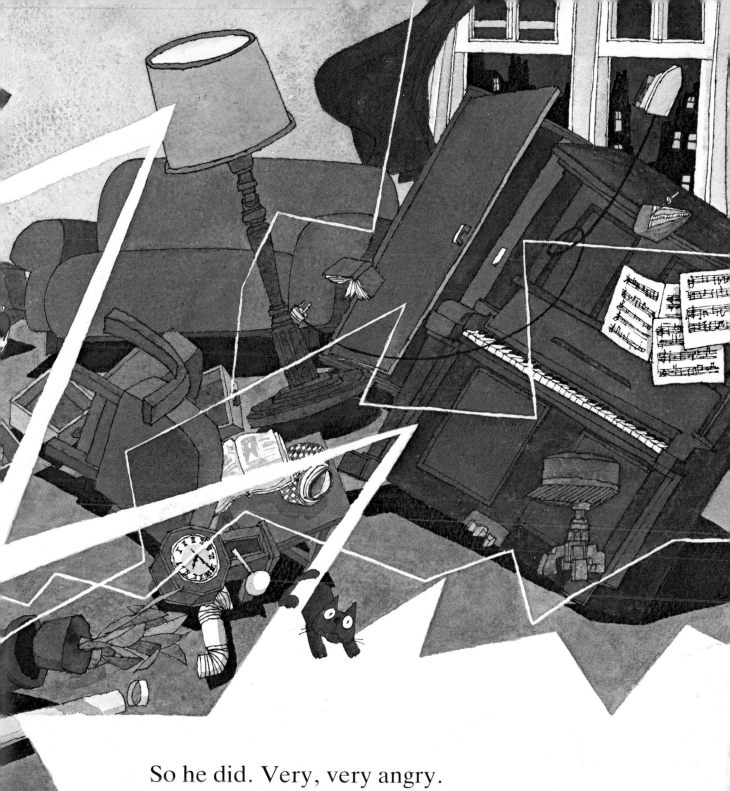

So he did. Very, very angry.
He got so angry that his anger became a dark cloud,
exploding into thunder and lightning and hailstones.

"That's enough,"
said his mother.
But it wasn't.

Arthur's anger became a hurricane, ripping off roofs
and chimneys and church steeples.

"That's enough,"
said his father.
But it wasn't.

Arthur's anger became a typhoon,
sweeping whole towns
into the sea.

"That's enough," said his grandfather.
But it wasn't.

Arthur's anger became an earth tremor. It split
the surface of the earth like a giant cracking an egg.
"That's enough," said his grandmother.
But it wasn't.

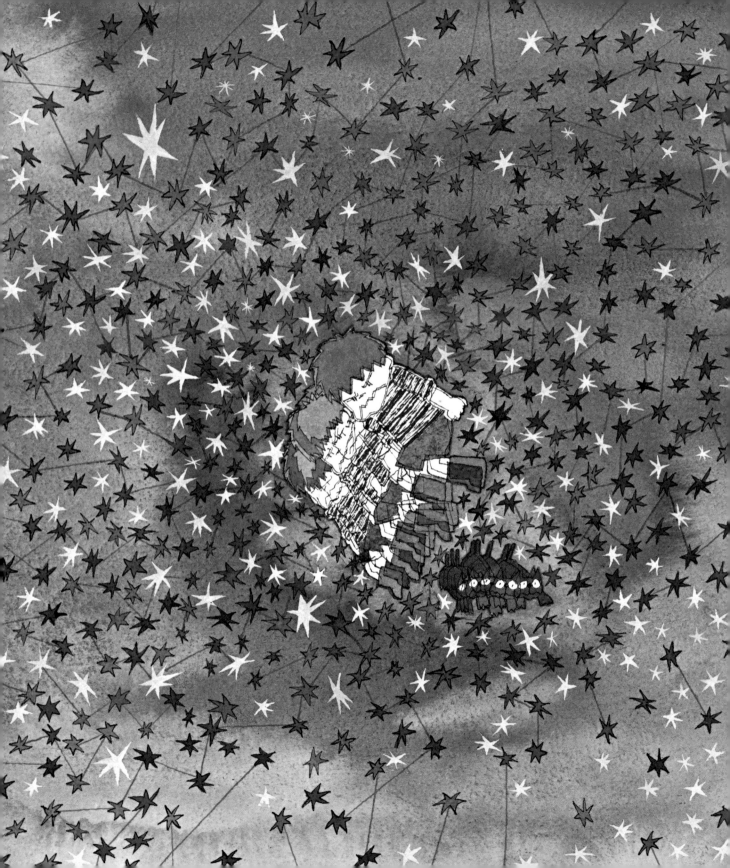

Arthur's anger became a universe-quake,

and the earth, the moon,

the stars, and the planets,

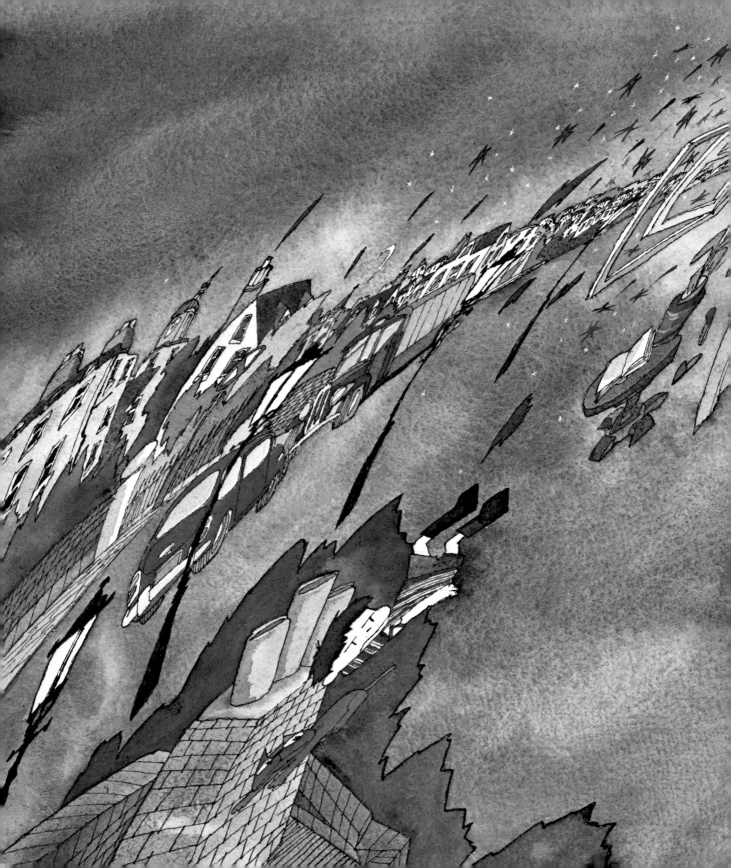

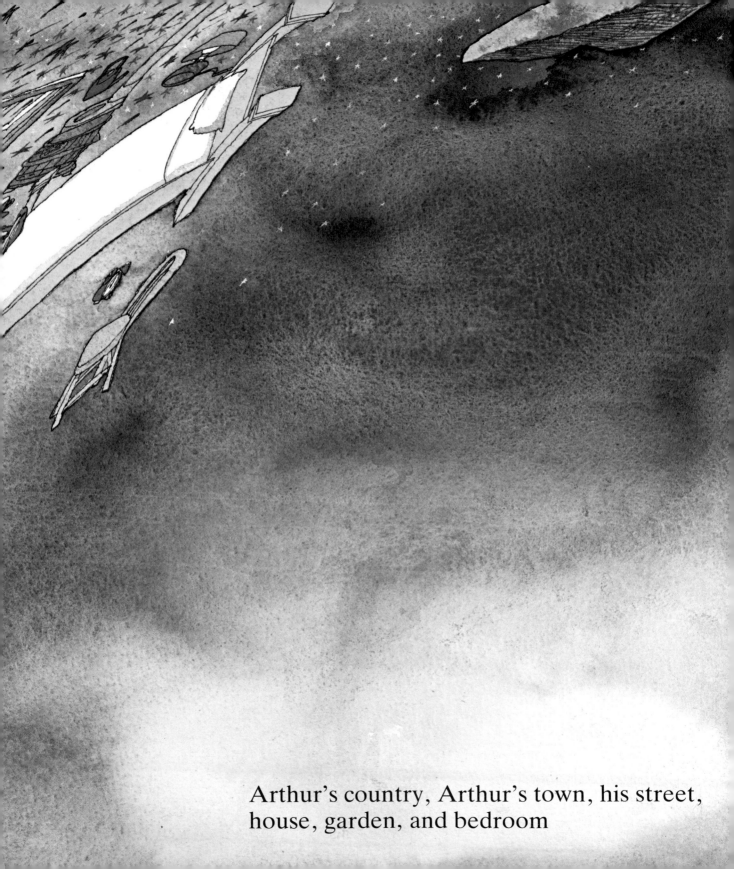

Arthur's country, Arthur's town, his street, house, garden, and bedroom

were nothing more
than specks
floating in space.

Arthur sat on a piece of Mars and thought.
He thought and thought.

"Why was I so angry?" he wondered.
He never could remember.
Can you?

for
Tremayne
and
Piers